Adapted by Nikki Grimes
Cover illustration by Robbin Cuddy
Interior illustrations by Don Williams, Jim Story, and H. R. Russell

A Random House PICTUREBACK® Book

Random House 🏠 New York

Copyright © 1993, 2002 Disney Enterprises, Inc. All rights reserved under International and Pan-American Copyright Conventions.
Published in the United States by Random House, Inc., New York, and simultaneously in Canada by Random House of Canada Limited, Toronto, in conjunction with Disney Enterprises, Inc.
Originally published in a slightly different form by Golden Books Publishing Company, Inc., in 1993.

Library of Congress Control Number: 2001088302
ISBN: 0-7364-1296-4
www.randomhouse.com/kids/disney
First Random House edition
Printed in the United States of America   July 2002   10 9 8 7 6 5

PICTUREBACK, RANDOM HOUSE, and the Random House colophon are registered trademarks of Random House, Inc.

Once upon a time, a wealthy widower lived in a fine
house with his daughter, Cinderella. He loved his daughter
very much and gave her many beautiful things. Still, he felt
Cinderella should have a mother's care, so he married a

woman with two young daughters who were just about
Cinderella's age.

Sadly, the gentleman died soon after, and Cinderella
discovered that her stepmother was a cold and cruel woman.

As the years passed, Cinderella's stepmother spoiled her two daughters. Anastasia and Drizella slept in large, lovely bedrooms, but Cinderella was given a tiny room in the attic. And while her stepsisters lived like princesses, poor Cinderella was forced to do laundry, serve meals, and clean house—just like a servant.

Still, Cinderella remained kind and gentle. All of the
animals loved her. She took special care of her dog, Bruno,
and brushed her old horse each day. The birds sang to her,
and the mice were always there to keep her company. She
made tiny clothes for them and often rescued them from the
claws of her stepmother's nasty cat, Lucifer.

Early one morning, Cinderella sat at the window in her tiny room and stared out at the castle in the distance. She dreamed of one day wearing a beautiful gown and dancing at a fancy ball. "Someday my dreams will come true," Cinderella said to herself.

Suddenly her stepmother called for her.

"Coming, Stepmother!" Cinderella answered.

Meanwhile, the King had his own troubles. He wanted his son to marry right away, but the Prince wanted to wait for the girl of his dreams.

The King had an idea. He told the Grand Duke they would have a ball and invite all the young women in the kingdom.

The invitations were delivered that very day.

"This just arrived from the palace," Cinderella said as she took the invitation from a messenger and handed it to her stepmother.

As their mother read the invitation aloud, Anastasia and Drizella jumped with excitement.

Cinderella asked if she could go, too.

"You may go," said her stepmother sternly, "if you finish all your chores and find something suitable to wear."

Cinderella ran to her room and found an old ball gown.
"Maybe it's a little old-fashioned, but I'll fix that," she
thought, looking at her pattern book.

But first she had chores to do. Cinderella started on them
right away, working as quickly as she could. But as soon as
she finished one task, she was given another.

It was eight o'clock at night when Cinderella completed the last chore. She dragged herself up to her dark room, tired and sad. There was no time left to finish her ball gown.

As she entered the room, her animal friends opened her closet doors. There hung her ball gown, finished to look just like the one in the pattern book. The birds and mice had done all the sewing.

"Oh, thank you so much!" Cinderella said.

Cinderella dressed and hurried downstairs to join her stepsisters. But when they saw that she wore a sash and beads that had once belonged to them, Anastasia and Drizella ripped the gown to shreds while their mother watched.

"Girls, girls," said their mother once the gown was ripped beyond repair. "That's enough. Hurry along now. Good night, Cinderella."

Sobbing, Cinderella ran into the garden.

"It's just no use," she cried. She thought her dreams would never come true.

Suddenly the garden filled with light, and Cinderella looked up to see her Fairy Godmother.

"Come now, dry those tears," the kind fairy said. "You can't go to the ball looking like that."

With a wave of her wand, the Fairy Godmother turned a pumpkin into a glittering coach and the mice into horses. She waved her wand again and changed the horse into a coachman and Bruno the dog into a footman. Last of all, she transformed Cinderella's rags into a lovely ball gown and put glass slippers on her tiny feet.

Cinderella twirled around in her beautiful new gown. "It's like a dream!" she said with a sigh.

"Yes, my child. But you'll only have until midnight," cautioned her Fairy Godmother. "On the stroke of twelve, the spell will be broken and everything will be as it was before."

Then Cinderella stepped into the coach and was whisked away to the ball.

When Cinderella entered the ballroom, the Prince rushed over and asked her to dance. Cinderella smiled and took his hand, never guessing that he was the Prince. They danced all night, and anyone could see that they were falling in love.

"Who is she, Mother?" asked Drizella. She hadn't recognized Cinderella, and neither had her mother.

Suddenly the clock began to strike twelve. "Oh, dear! It's midnight! I must leave," said Cinderella, breaking away from the Prince.

"Wait! I don't even know your name! How will I find you?" called the Prince. But Cinderella could hear the clock still striking, and she ran out of the ballroom.

The Grand Duke ran after her. He knew the Prince had finally found the girl he wanted to marry, and the King would be furious if she got away.

Racing down the stairs, Cinderella lost a glass slipper. The Grand Duke, a few steps behind, stopped to pick it up. When he looked around a moment later, she was gone.

Just beyond the palace gates, at the last stroke of midnight, the spell was broken. Just as the Fairy Godmother had said, all was as it had been before. All, that is, except for the tiny glass slipper on Cinderella's foot. She took the slipper off and carried it home.

The next day the King was frantic. "The Prince is determined to marry none but the girl who fits this slipper," the Grand Duke told him.

When Cinderella's stepmother heard the news, she decided that Cinderella must not have the chance to try on the slipper. She quickly locked the girl in her room. But Cinderella wasn't locked in for long. The mice stole the key, carried it upstairs, and slipped it under Cinderella's door.

Anastasia and Drizella tried to force their big feet into the tiny slipper, but it was no use.

Then, just as the Grand Duke was about to leave, Cinderella appeared at the top of the stairs. "May I try it on?" she asked.

The footman carried the slipper toward Cinderella, but her stepmother stuck out her cane and tripped him! The glass slipper crashed down onto the floor, shattering into a thousand pieces.

The Grand Duke was horrified.

"But I have the other slipper," Cinderella said with a smile, pulling the glass slipper from under her apron.

The Grand Duke knelt before Cinderella and eased the slipper onto her dainty foot. It was a perfect fit!

Soon Cinderella and the Prince were married. And they lived happily ever after.